Ms. Wiz Spells Trouble

Titles in the *Ms. Wiz* series

Ms. Wiz
Spells
Trouble

by Terence Blacker

illustrations by Tony Ross

Marshall Cavendish Children

For Alice

Text copyright © Terence Blacker 1988
Illustrations copyright © Tony Ross 1966
First published 1988 by Piccadilly Press, London
This edition published by arrangement with Andersen Press Ltd., London

Marshall Cavendish Corporation
99 White Plains Road
Tarrytown, NY 10591
www.marshallcavendish.us/kids

Library of Congress Cataloging-in-Publication Data

Blacker, Terence.
Ms. Wiz spells trouble / by Terence Blacker ; illustrated by Toni Ross. — 1st ed.
p. cm.
Summary: A mysterious new teacher, thought by some to be a witch, changes the worst class in the school into the best with some strange and wonderful tricks.
ISBN 978-0-7614-5548-6
[1. Teachers—Fiction. 2. Schools—Fiction. 3. Witches—Fiction. 4. Magic—Fiction.] I. Ross, Tony, ill. II. Title.
PZ7.B53225Ms 2008
[Fic]—dc22
2008004108

Designer: Anahid Hamparian

Printed in China
First Marshall Cavendish edition, 2008
1 3 5 6 4 2

Marshall Cavendish
Children

Chapter One
A New Arrival

Most teachers are strange and the teachers at St. Barnabas School were no exception.

Yet it's almost certain that none of them – not Mr. Gilbert, the head teacher, who liked to pick his nose during Assembly, not Mrs. Hicks who talked to her teddies in class, not Miss Gomaz who smoked cigarettes in the lavatory – *none* of them was quite as odd as Class Three's new teacher.

Some of the children in Class Three thought she was a witch. Others said she was a hippy. A few of them thought she was just a bit mad. But they all agreed that there had never been anyone quite like her at St. Barnabas before.

This is her story. I wonder what *you* think she was . . .

As soon as their new teacher walked into the classroom on the first day of term, the children of Class Three sensed that there was something different about her. She was quite tall, with long black hair and bright green eyes. She wore tight jeans and a purple blouse. Her fingers were decorated with several large rings and black nail varnish. She looked as if she were on her way to a disco, not teaching at a school.

Most surprising of all, she wasn't frightened. Class Three was known in the school as the "problem class." It had a reputation for being difficult and noisy, for having what was called a "disruptive element." Miss Jones, their last teacher, had left the school in tears. But none of that seemed to

worry this strange-looking new teacher.

"My name is Miss Wisdom," she said in a quiet but firm voice. "So what do you say to me every morning when I walk in?"

"Good morning, Miss Wisdom," said Class Three unenthusiastically.

"Wrong," said the teacher with a flash of her green eyes. "You say 'Hi, Ms. Wiz!' "

Jack, who was one of Class Three's Disruptive Element, giggled at the back of the class.

"Yo," he said in a silly American accent. "Why, hi Ms. Wiz!"

Caroline, the class dreamer, was paying attention for a change.

"Why is it Ms. . . . er, Ms. ?" she asked.

"Well," said Ms. Wiz, "I'm not a Mrs. because I'm not married, thank goodness, and I'm not Miss because I think Miss sounds silly for a grown woman, don't you?"

"Not as silly as Ms.," muttered Katrina, who liked to find fault wherever possible.

"And why Wiz?" asked a rather large boy sitting in the front row. It was Podge, who was probably the most annoying and certainly the greediest boy in the class.

"Wiz?" said Ms. Wiz with a mysterious smile. "Just you wait and see."

Ms. Wiz reached inside a big leather bag that she had placed beside her desk. She pulled out a china cat.

"That," she said, placing the cat carefully on her desk, "is my friend Hecate the Cat. She's watching you all the time. She sees everything and hears everything. She's my spy."

Ms. Wiz turned to the blackboard.

"Weird," muttered Jack.

An odd, hissing sound came from

the china cat. Its eyes lit up like
torches.

"Hecate sees you even when my
back is turned," said Ms. Wiz, who
now faced the class. "Will the person
who said 'weird' spell it please?"

Everyone stared at Jack, who
blushed.

"I.T.," he stammered.

No one laughed.

"Er, W . . . I . . ."

"Wrong," said Ms. Wiz. "W.E.I.R.D.

If you don't know how to spell a word, Jack, don't use it." She patted the china cat.

"Good girl, Hecate," she said.

"How did she know my name?" whispered Jack.

The new teacher smiled. "Children, remember one thing. Ms. Wiz knows everything."

"Now," she said briskly. "Pay attention, please. Talking of spelling, I'm going to give you a first lesson in casting spells."

"Oh great," said Katrina grumpily. "Now we've got a witch for a teacher."

Hecate the Cat hissed angrily.

"No, Katrina, not a witch," said Ms. Wiz sharply. "We don't call them witches these days. It gives people the wrong idea. We call them Paranormal Operatives. Now – any suggestions for our first spell?"

Podge put up his hand immediately.

"Could we turn our crayons into lollipops, please Ms.?" he asked.

"No," said Ms. Wiz. "Spells are not for personal greed."

"How about turning Class Two into frogs?" asked Katrina.

"Nor are they for revenge. There will be no unpleasant spells around here while I'm your teacher," said Ms. Wiz before adding, almost as an

afterthought, "unless they're deserved, of course."

She looked out of the window. In the playground Mr. Brown, the school caretaker, was sweeping up leaves.

"Please draw the playground," said Ms. Wiz. "Imagine it without any leaves. The best picture will create the spell."

Almost for the first time in living memory, Class Three worked in complete quiet. Katrina didn't

complain that someone had nicked her pencil. Caroline managed to concentrate on her work. Podge forgot to look in his trouser pocket for one last sweet. Not a single paper pellet was shot across the room by Jack.

At the end of the lesson, Ms. Wiz looked at the drawings carefully.

"Well, they're all quite good," she said eventually. "But I think I like Caroline's the best."

She took Caroline's drawing and carefully taped it to the window.

"Please close your eyes while I cast the spell," she said.

There was a curious humming noise as Class Three sat, eyes closed, in silence.

"Open," said Ms. Wiz, after a few seconds. "Regard Caroline's work."

The children looked at Caroline's drawing. It was steaming slightly and, in one corner, there was a freshly drawn pile of leaves.

"Hey – look at the playground!" shouted Katrina.

Everyone looked out of the window. To their amazement, the leaves on the ground had disappeared. Mr. Brown stood by his wheelbarrow, scratching his head.

"Weird," said Jack. "Very weird indeed."

Chapter Two
"Ms. Wiz is Magic"

"Yes, I'm afraid she is a bit odd,"
sighed the head teacher, Mr. Gilbert,
as he took tea one morning with Miss
Gomaz and Mrs. Hicks in the Staff
Common Room.

"Those jeans," sniffed Miss Gomaz.
"And I never thought I'd live to
see *black* nail-varnish at St. Barnabas."

"But you have to admit she seems
to have Class Three under control,"
said Mr. Gilbert. "That's a whole week
she's been here and not one child has
been sent to my study. Not one
window has been broken."

Mrs. Hicks stirred her tea
disapprovingly.

"It won't last," she said. "The
Disruptive Element will get the better
of her. And there are some very

12

strange noises coming from that classroom."

"I'd keep an eye on the situation if I were you, head teacher," said Miss Gomaz.

Mr. Gilbert sighed.

"Yes," he said wearily. "That's what I'll do. Keep an eye on the situation."

The fact is that Class Three, including the Disruptive Element, were having the time of their lives.

Every lesson with Ms. Wiz was different.

"Now, Class Three," she would say, "I'm going to teach you something rather unusual. But remember – what happens in this classroom is our secret. The magic only works if nobody except us knows about it."

Surprisingly, Class Three agreed.

So no one – not even parents or

other children at the school – had any idea of the strange things that happened to Class Three.

They never heard how Caroline's picture of the playground saved Mr. Brown a morning's work.

They never heard how Jack's desk moved to the front of the class all by itself when Hecate spotted him talking at the back.

They never heard how Katrina flew around the class three times on a

vacuum cleaner after she had complained that Ms. Wiz couldn't be a real witch – sorry, Paranormal Operative – because she didn't ride a broomstick.

They never heard about the nature lesson when the class met Herbert, a pet rat that Ms. Wiz kept up her sleeve.

But they did hear about the day when Podge became the hero of the class.

Nobody could keep *that* a secret.

Once every term, Class Three played a soccer match against a team from a school nearby, called Brackenhurst. It was a very important game and everyone from St. Barnabas gathered in the playground to watch. Last term, Class Three had lost 10–0.

"That was because Miss Jones

picked all the wimps," explained Jack.

"Because she was a wimp herself," said Caroline.

The rest of the class agreed noisily.

"*I'll* be manager," shouted Jack over the din.

Ms. Wiz held up her hands like a wizard about to cast a spell.

"I'll be manager," she said firmly.

"But you don't know anything about soccer," said Jack.

"Ms. Wiz knows everything," said Caroline.

"Creep!" muttered Katrina.

Hecate the Cat hissed angrily.

"All right, Hecate," said Katrina quickly. "I take it back."

"My team," said Ms. Wiz, "is Jack, Simon, Katrina, Alex and . . ."

She looked around the classroom and saw Podge's arm waving wildly.

"*No*, Ms. Wiz," several of the class

17

shouted at once. "Not Podge! He's useless!"

". . . and Podge."

There was a groan from around the classroom.

"Here comes another hammering," said Jack gloomily.

For a while during the game that afternoon, it looked as though Jack's prediction had been right. After three minutes, Brackenhurst had already scored twice. Podge had been a disaster, falling over his own feet every time the ball came near him.

"Serves that Ms. Cleverclogs right," said Mrs. Hicks, who was watching the match with Miss Gomaz. "Look at her, jumping up and down like that, making herself look foolish in front of the kiddies. Anybody would think she was a child herself."

"It's embarrassing, that's what it

is," agreed Miss Gomaz.

"*Do* something," said Caroline who was standing next to Ms. Wiz.

"And what do you suggest, Caroline?" asked Ms. Wiz whose normally pale face was now quite red.

"You know," whispered Caroline. "Something *special*."

"Oh, all right," sighed Ms. Wiz. "I suppose a *little* magic wouldn't hurt."

At that moment, Podge blundered

into one of the Brackenhurst's
players and knocked him over. Mr.
Gilbert, who was referee, blew hard
on his whistle for a free kick against
Class Three – but not a sound came
out. In fact, the only sound to be heard
was a faint humming noise from the
direction of Ms. Wiz.

"That's better," said Caroline.

Brackenhurst's players were still
waiting for the whistle to blow when
Podge set off with the ball at his feet.
He took two paces and booted it
wildly. It was heading several feet
wide of the Brackenhurst goal when,
to everyone's astonishment, the ball
changed direction and, as if it had a
life of its own, flew into the back of
the net.

For a moment, there was a stunned
silence. Then Ms. Wiz could be heard
cheering on her team once more.

"What a shot!" she shouted. "Nice
one, Podge!"

"Appalling behavior," muttered Mrs. Hicks.

From then on, the game altered completely. Not even in his wildest dreams, when he had scored the winning goal for Spurs in the FA Cup Final, had Podge played so well.

Soon even Jack was shouting, "Give it to Podge! Give the ball to Podge!" while the Brackenhurst players were screaming, "Stop the fat one! Trip him, someone!"

But nobody could stop Podge. Playing as if he were under a spell, he scored three goals to give Class Three a great 3–2 victory.

After the game, the class gathered around Ms. Wiz, shouting, cheering, and singing songs.

"So much for her having her class under control," said Mrs. Hicks. "They may win matches but Class Three are worse than ever with the new teacher."

Miss Gomaz had hurried over to Mr. Gilbert.

"Just look at that, head teacher," she said, pointing to Class Three, who were now singing "Ms. Wiz is magic!" at the top of their voices. "It's nothing short of anarchy."

But Mr. Gilbert wasn't listening. He was still studying his new whistle and wondering why it hadn't worked.

Chapter Three
An Extremely Mathematical Owl

"This is all very difficult," said Mr. Gilbert, puffing nervously on his pipe. He was sitting in his study with Ms. Wiz, who at this moment was looking at him with an annoying little smile on her face. "Very awkward. You see, Miss Wisdom – er, Ms. Wiz – there have been, well, complaints."

"Goodness," said Ms. Wiz brightly. "What on earth about?"

Mr. Gilbert fumbled around with his pipe. Why *was* he feeling so nervous? Of course, he was always uneasy with women, but there were lots of women who were more frightening than Ms. Wiz – Mrs. Gilbert, for a start. The thought of his wife made the head teacher sit up in

24

his armchair and try again.

"Firstly, there have been complaints about the way you look," he said, glancing at Ms. Wiz. She was actually wearing black lipstick today.

"You find something wrong with the way I look?" asked Ms. Wiz, who was beginning to be confused by this conversation.

"No, no," said Mr. Gilbert, tapping his pipe on an ashtray. "I like . . . I mean, I don't . . . personally . . . Then," he said, quickly changing the subject, "there's what you teach. Your history lessons, for example."

"But Class Three loves history," said Ms. Wiz. "We're doing the French Revolution at the moment."

"So I gather," said Mr. Gilbert. "The entire class was walking around the playground yesterday shouting, 'Behead the aristocrats!' I'm told that Jack was carrying a potato on the end of a sharp stick."

Ms. Wiz laughed. "They're very keen," she said.

"Perhaps you could move on to some other part of history – *nice history*," said the head teacher. "1066, the Armada, King Alfred and the cakes."

"Oh no," said Ms. Wiz. "We already have our next project."

"May I know what it is?" asked Mr. Gilbert uneasily.

"Certainly," said Ms. Wiz. "The Great Fire of London."

The head teacher gulped. Mrs. Hicks and Miss Gomaz had been right. Ms. Wiz spelt trouble.

"Perhaps," he said, "you could concentrate on some other subject for the time being."

"Of course," said Ms. Wiz. "We'll try a spot of maths for a while."

Mr. Gilbert smiled for the first time that morning.

"Perfect," he said.

Maths, he thought to himself after Ms. Wiz had left his study. That couldn't cause trouble. Could it?

"Now, Class Three," said Ms. Wiz that afternoon. "I'm going to test you on your nine times table – multiplication and division."

There was a groan around the classroom. Nobody liked the nine times table.

"And to help me," continued Ms. Wiz, "I've brought my friend Archimedes." She reached inside her desk and brought out a large white owl. "Archie's what they call a bit of a number-cruncher. He loves his tables," she said, putting the owl on top of the blackboard.

"Cats, rats and now owls," muttered Katrina. "This place gets more like a zoo every day."

"Archie is a barn owl," said Ms.

Wiz, ignoring Katrina. "An extremely mathematical barn owl. Place the wastepaper basket beneath him please, Caroline."

"Why, Ms. Wiz?" asked Caroline.

"Wait and see," said Ms. Wiz.

Caroline put the wastepaper basket beneath Archie who was now looking around the classroom, blinking wisely.

"Now Podge," said Ms. Wiz. "Tell Archie what five nines are."

"Forty-five," said Podge.

"Toowoo," went Archie.

"That means correct," said Ms. Wiz. "Simon – nine nines."

"Eighty one," said Simon.

"Toowoo."

"Now Jack," said Ms. Wiz. "Let's try division. A boy has 108 marbles He divides them among his nine friends. What does that make?"

"It makes him a wally for giving away all his marbles," said Jack.

Archie looked confused.

"Try again, Jack," said Ms. Wiz patiently.

"Erm . . . eleven."

Class Three looked at Archie expectantly. Without a sound, the owl lifted its tail and did something very nasty into the wastepaper basket beneath him.

"Uuuuuuuurrrrggghhhh, gross," said the children. "He's done a—"

"The correct word is guano," said Ms. Wiz. "Jack?"

"Ten," said Jack.

Archie lifted his tail.

"Eight."

Archie did it again.

"How does he keep doing that?" asked Podge.

Ms. Wiz shrugged. "He's well trained," she said.

"We'd better have another basket standing by," said Katrina. "Jack's never going to get it."

"He'd better," said Ms. Wiz firmly. "Every time Archie is obliged to do his . . . guano, it means fifty lines."

Jack groaned. "Um . . ."

Outside the door Mrs. Hicks and Miss Gomaz were listening carefully.

They had left their classes with some reading work and were determined to catch the new teacher doing something wrong.

"Listen to that noise," said Miss Gomaz. "It's an absolute disgrace."

"Let's take a look through the window from the playground," said Mrs. Hicks.

Moments later, the two teachers were watching in amazement as Jack struggled to give Archie the correct answer.

"There's a bird on the blackboard," whispered Miss Gomaz.

"It's . . . it's going to the lavatory,"

gasped Mrs. Hicks. "In a bin. I can't believe my eyes."

They were just pressing their noses to the windowpane to get a closer look when Ms. Wiz glanced up. Those at the front of the class could hear a slight hum coming from her direction.

"Miss Gomaz! Miss Gomaz!" said Mrs. Hicks. "My nose! It's stuck to the glass!"

"Mine too!" cried Miss Gomaz,

trying to pull back from the window-pane. "Ouch! That hurts!"

It was at that moment that the bell rang for afternoon break. Soon the teachers were surrounded by laughing children.

"Don't just stand there, you horrible children," screamed Mrs. Hicks. "Get help quickly!"

"No need," said Ms. Wiz, who had joined the children in the playground. She tapped the glass. Miss Gomaz and Mrs. Hicks fell back, free at last.

"It must have been the frost," said Ms. Wiz, with an odd little smile.

"Frost?" said Miss Gomaz, rubbing her nose. "At this time of year? Don't talk daft."

"It's only September," said Mrs. Hicks.

"Yes," said Ms. Wiz. "What funny old weather we've been having, don't you think?"

Chapter Four
Herbert Takes a Wrong Turn

It was during an art lesson that Class Three were first given an idea where Ms. Wiz came from.

She had asked the children to draw an imaginary building. The project was called "The House of My Dreams."

Jack drew a house that looked like Wembley Stadium. It had a soccer pitch in the living room and all the walls were slanted like skateboard ramps.

Caroline drew the mansion that she would have when she became a film star. It had a huge lawn and swimming pool. In every room, there was a cocktail cabinet for drinks.

Podge drew Buckingham Palace

made out of milk chocolate and fudge.

Katrina drew a strange, dark cottage in a wood. Cats with shining eyes stood guard on each side of the front door and bats flew in and out of its old thatched roof. She called it "Ms. Wiz's Magic Cottage."

When Katrina finished the picture, Ms. Wiz laughed. "It's lovely," she said, "but not at all like where I really live."

"Where *do* you live?" asked Katrina. The entire class grew quiet. Somehow no one had ever dared ask Ms. Wiz about herself before.

"I live in a flat a long, long way away," said Ms. Wiz. "At a place where almost certainly none of you have been. It's on the outskirts of town."

"Can we come and visit you during the holidays?" asked Jack.

"During the holidays I'm doing

36

other things," said Ms. Wiz. "That's my job – to go wherever a little magic is needed. Wherever," she smiled, "things need shaking up a little."

"You've certainly shaken things up at St. Barnabas," said Katrina. "Does that mean you'll be leaving us soon?"

Ms. Wiz smiled. "Katrina, I'll only leave you when you no longer need me."

For a moment, there was silence in Class Three. Then Podge put up his hand.

"If you live so far away," he asked, "how do you get to school every day? Do you fly on your vacuum cleaner?"

"No," said Ms. Wiz. "I come by bus."

If Ms. Wiz was a little more serious than usual that afternoon, it was because she was thinking of the evening ahead of her. It was Parents' Evening.

Ms. Wiz liked being with children. She didn't even mind being with teachers. But the idea of a whole evening spent in the company of parents made her feel tired already.

"I must remember to keep my spells under control," she said to herself as she waited for the first parent to arrive. "Adults aren't like children. Magic seems to upset them."

The door opened.

"I'm Harris," said a large man in a suit, who was the first parent to arrive. He shook Ms. Wiz firmly by the hand. "Peter's dad. This," he nodded curtly towards a nervous-looking woman standing a pace behind him, "is Mother."

Peter? Ms. Wiz's mind raced. Who was Peter? Of course – that was Podge's real name.

"Pod – I mean Peter is doing well

this term," she said, glancing at her notes.

"We're not happy," said Mr. Harris firmly. "Isn't that right, Mother?"

"It is," said Mrs. Harris. "We're not happy at all."

"The lad's gone strange on us," continued Mr. Harris. "Always got his head in a book. Or talking about school. Asking us questions about this and that when his mother and I are trying to watch telly."

"Questions all the time," said Mrs. Harris.

"Yak yak yak," said Mr. Harris. "I'm a busy man. I work at the Town Hall. I want to relax of an evening, not answer questions from my own flesh and blood. That's your job."

Ms. Wiz smiled. "Perhaps it's a good sign that he's interested in—"

"He's never been interested before. Tea, telly, bed was our way. Nothing wrong with that." Mr. Harris leant forward angrily. "I've said to Mother and I'll say it to you. I smell a rat –" (for a horrible moment, Ms. Wiz thought he had discovered Herbert, who was asleep up her sleeve) – "and when Cuthbert Harris smells a rat, heads will roll. Come on, Mother, I'm off."

Mr. Harris stood up and, without another word, walked towards the door. Was it an accident that a banana skin had been left on the floor – or was it a touch of Ms. Wiz's magic after all?

"Woooaaaahhh!"

With a sickening crash, Mr. Harris landed on the floor in a heap.

"Oh, Cuthbert!" said Mrs. Harris. "Your best suit!"

Podge's father stood up, red-faced.

"Right! That's it!" he said as he dusted himself down. "Town Hall's going to hear of this. Heads will roll!"

Ms. Wiz sighed as the door slammed behind Mr. and Mrs. Harris. Yes, she definitely preferred children to parents.

Ms. Wiz was not often angry but when, a few days after Parents' Evening, Mr. Gilbert brought a School Inspector from the Town Hall into the classroom, there was an unusual sharpness in her tone when she addressed the class.

41

"Now sit up, Class Three," she said after the head teacher had left the School Inspector sitting at a little desk at the back of the class. "Remember we're being inspected today."

The School Inspector pursed his lips and made a note on the pad in front of him.

It was a quiet lesson without, of course, a hint of magic. Even Hecate the Cat remained hidden in Ms. Wiz's bag.

Unfortunately nobody had told Herbert that Class Three was being inspected and Herbert, as luck would have it, decided at this particular moment to explore the classroom.

After a few minutes of the lesson, he had discovered a new tunnel. It was warm and dark, like a very inviting, old-fashioned chimney.

Who could blame him for wanting to explore it? Rats like chimneys.

How was he to know that he was
climbing up the left leg of the School
Inspector's trousers?

At first the School Inspector
twitched. Then he shifted nervously
in his seat. Then, as Herbert edged his
way past his knee and upwards, the
School Inspector stood up.

"Oh . . . ooh . . . ," he said, patting
his thigh. "What the . . . oh . . . ah . . ."
He hopped around the classroom.

It was then that Herbert decided

the chimney was moving around
rather too much for comfort – and
made for the safety of the School
Inspector's underpants.

"AAAARRRRRGGGGGHHHHH!"

The School Inspector tore at his
belt, jumped out of his trousers, and
ran from the classroom.

Class Three watched in amazement
as the half-naked figure sprinted
across the playground, out of the
school gates, and down the road.

Relieved that the earthquake had passed, Herbert emerged nervously from the School Inspector's trousers on the classroom floor.

"Oh, Herbert," said Ms. Wiz. "You've done it now."

Chapter Five
An Absolute Disgrace

Mr. Gilbert was in a muddle. You might think that Mr. Gilbert was always in a muddle, but this was the biggest muddle he had ever been in since he became head teacher of St. Barnabas.

He was in such a muddle that his bald head had developed ugly red blotches. His attention would wander during lessons. He had even stopped picking his nose during Assembly.

"I'm on the horns of a dilemma," he told Mrs. Gilbert one evening. "People keep telling me that Ms. Wiz is a disaster. Miss Gomaz and Mrs. Hicks say she's a troublemaker. The School Inspector says her classroom is a health hazard. Mr. Harris says heads will roll. They all want me to suspend her before the end-of-term prizegiving next week."

"Suspend her then, Henry," said Mrs. Gilbert. "What's the problem?"

"The problem is that the children of Class Three have won all the prizes this term. It's incredible. That sleepy Caroline has won the Art Prize. The A for Attitude Award for Good Behavior has gone to Katrina of all people. Even the appalling Podge has won a Commendation for his story, 'The Enchanted Fudge Cake with a Thick Creamy Milk Chocolate Filling.' How on earth can I say, 'Well done everyone in Class Three and by the way I'm suspending your teacher'?"

"You'd better do what you think is best," said Mrs. Gilbert. "But don't allow yourself to be bullied this time."

"Of course not," said Mr. Gilbert. "You know where I stand on bullying."

"Let me guess," said Mrs. Gilbert. "On the horns of a dilemma?"

"Precisely," said Mr. Gilbert.

"It is true that you're going to be suspended?" asked Katrina the next day in class. "Ever since the School Inspector lost his trousers, Mr. Gilbert's been giving you some very funny looks."

"So have Miss Gomaz and Mrs. Hicks," said Jack. "They look positively happy."

"My dad's smiling a lot," said Podge. "And that's never a good sign."

"Never you mind about me," said Ms. Wiz. "I can look after myself."

"Yeah," said Simon. "You can magic 'em. That would show 'em."

"What have I always said? No unpleasant spells," said Ms. Wiz.

"Oh, Ms. ," said Podge. "Couldn't

49

you just use a bit of magic – just one little spell on Mr. Gilbert?"

"Maybe you could change him into a human being," suggested Jack.

There were cheers around the classroom. Ms. Wiz held up her hands. Class Three were quiet.

"No," she said. "I refuse to listen to rumors. If the head teacher no longer requires my services, there's nothing to be done about it."

"Oh yes, there is," said Jack.

Which is how Class Three's Great Plan came into being.

End-of-term prizegiving was the most important event of the term for St. Barnabas. It took place on the last day before the holidays, and everybody was there.

On the platform in the School Hall sat Mr. Gilbert, the School Inspector, all the teachers and the Lady

Mayoress, a large, impressive woman who was wearing a large, impressive hat. In the audience were the children with their parents.

Mr. Gilbert had just finished his end-of-term speech which, give or take a couple of pathetic jokes, was the same as every end-of-term speech he had made for the last ten years.

"Now," he said, "I would like to ask the Lady Mayoress—" Mr. Gilbert gave a simpering little bow in her direction "—to present the prizes. First, the Art Prize to Caroline Smith of Class Three."

There was polite applause as Caroline collected her prize.

"The Maths Prize has been won by Jack Beddows of Class Three."

Jack collected his prize, giving a modest wave to his supporters from the platform.

"The A for Attitude Award for Good Behavior—" Mr. Gilbert tried to

keep the disbelief out of his voice, "to Katrina O'Brien of Class Three." Katrina actually gave a little curtsey to the Lady Mayoress as she was presented with her award.

"And Specially Commended for his essay, 'The Enchanted Fudge Cake with a Thick Creamy Milk Chocolate Filling' – Peter Harris of Class Three."

Podge climbed the steps to the platform. But instead of collecting his prize from the Lady Mayoress, he took the microphone from the astonished head teacher.

"Everyone in Class Three wants to thank Ms. Wiz," he announced. "She's the best teacher we've ever had—"

"Give me that microphone, boy," said Mr. Gilbert, chasing Podge around the stage.

"WE HOPE SHE NEVER EVER LEAVES!" shouted Podge. "Don't we, Class Three?"

At that moment, the children of Class Three stood up and started cheering. Several of them produced banners, reading "MS. WIZ IS MAGIC" and "NO SACK FOR MS. WIZ," which had been smuggled into the hall.

"You can stop that right now, Peter," said Podge's father, Mr. Harris, advancing towards the platform. "I'm going to give you a proper larruping when you get home."

There was a humming sound from the back of the stage where Ms. Wiz was sitting quietly.

Suddenly Mr. Harris had turned into a strange pig-like animal.

"Goodness," said Miss Gomaz. "He's turned into a warthog."

"Surely not," said Mrs. Hicks. "Warthogs don't have those funny little tusks. He looks more like a wild boar to me."

"Never mind that," shouted Mr.

Gilbert. "We have a full-scale riot on our baaa—" In a flash, there was a sheep standing in the head teacher's place.

By now the entire school was chanting, "We want Ms. Wiz! We want Ms. Wiz!"

Ms. Wiz stood up and Podge gave her the microphone.

"I think," she said firmly, "that we should continue Prizegiving in half an hour. I'd like to see Class Three in their classroom now, please."

She made her way through the audience, which was now silent.

"Phone the police, Miss Gomaz," hissed Mrs. Hicks.

Ms. Wiz glanced over her shoulder.

Suddenly where Miss Gomaz and Mrs. Hicks had been standing, there were two grey geese, making a furious gobbling noise.

*

"That was very kind of you, Class Three," said Ms. Wiz, when all the children had gathered in the classroom. "But the fact is, I'm leaving St. Barnabas anyway."

There was silence in the classroom.

"Why?" asked Katrina eventually.

"After all that," muttered Podge.

"I go where magic is needed," said Ms. Wiz. "Where things need livening up. Today you've proved that you no

longer need me. You're the best class in the school."

"We won't be, without you," said Caroline.

"Yes, you will," said Ms. Wiz. "Wait and see."

"We'll miss you," said Jack, serious for once.

"No, you won't because . . ."

The class looked expectantly at Ms. Wiz. Caroline managed to stop sniffling at the back of the class.

". . . because I'll be back," said Ms. Wiz.

"When?"

"Where?"

"Next term?"

Ms. Wiz held up her hands.

"I'll come back and see each one of you," she said with a smile. "When you least expect it, when you need a spot of Ms. Wiz in your life, I'll be there."

"Every one of us?" asked Simon.

"Every one of you," said Ms. Wiz. "And I'll bring Hecate the Cat and Herbert."

Ms. Wiz gathered up her bag. She swung her leg over her vacuum cleaner, like a cowboy about to ride out of town on his horse.

"Go back to the School Hall and finish prizegiving," she said. "You'll find everything's back to normal."

Ms. Wiz hovered in mid-air by the classroom window.

"See you soon, Class Three," she said and flew off across the playground and over the School Hall.

"Oh no," said Jack as the class filed back into the hall. "Look who Ms. Wiz has forgotten."

On the platform beside Mr. Gilbert, the School Inspector and the Lady Mayoress, who were looking as if nothing strange had happened at all, stood two grey geese.

"She'll *have* to come back now," said Katrina.

"No unpleasant spells," said Podge.

They heard a familiar hum from outside the hall.

"Gobble gobble gobble – absolute disgrace," said Miss Gomaz.

Jack sighed.

"I think I preferred them as geese," he said.